Fighting To Let Go

Fighting For Love Series Prequel

Aaliyah Rose

Free Gift

Enjoyed this book and want to stay in touch?

Join my Readers Club to receive my newsletter with the latest updates on my book releases and receive FREE books. You can unsubscribe at any time. Get on board here to join me or click the image below.

https://www.subscribepage.com/aaliyahrosero-mance_free

Follow her on Facebook: @AaliyahRoseRomance

https://www.facebook.com/
AaliyahRoseRomance

To all my fans who love my books, who continue to inspire me to write, and who challenge me to create new worlds...

Thank you
xo

Contents

Chapter One

Jodi

Have you ever wondered if something was missing from your life?

It was the same question that had plagued Jodi for months. A constant thought that had been on her mind for the past year, and caused her to get lost in more questions of '*What is it?*' and '*Could it be…?*'

Troubled, Jodi drummed her fingernails on the tabletop as she took another spoonful of her chicken caesar salad. It was a quiet night and the spirits of the staff and patients seemed to be subdued. It had been a busy day and looking around the staffroom at the handful of other nurses and doctors, it was evident each carried the usual worries and concerns that the work of the day presented.

Jodi looked up at the clock. Only 11:39pm. She exhaled a slow deep breath. *Just two hours to go.* She took another bite of salad, looking out the window despondently.

"Still here Jodi? I thought your shift ended an hour ago?" the familiar voice interrupted the silence. Jodi looked up to see Dr. Dixon smiling down at her. "Mind if I sit?"

Dr. John Dixon was what the other women around the hospital termed a George Clooney twin. Just a younger, blonde version, a bit taller and broader but sporting the same neatly trimmed stubble on that defined jawline.

Jodi swallowed her food, "Of course" she waved her fork at the seat across from her "Please, sit." Even though she much preferred to sit on her own in silence, she couldn't deny a friendly face, especially John's.

Dr. Dixon had helped her immensely when she had first transferred to the new hospital in Los Angeles two years ago. She had known no one there and he had been kind enough to show her around. In the few chances they ended up in surgery together, he had explained every detail of the operations, carefully pointing out the intricacies of the human body's anatomy. Now, due to his tutelage, she was quite the competent surgical assistant.

John placed his dinner on the table, took a seat and carefully removed the hot cover over his plate to reveal a steaming hot lasagna. He grinned across the table at her as he lightly fanned his dinner. A grin that most girls would swoon under. All pearly whites, chiseled jaw and that sparkle in his eyes.

"So, what are you still doing here?" He took a forkful and blew on the food before placing it in his mouth.

Jodi sighed. "I told Stacy that I would cover the rest of her shift for her. Some family emergency again."

"I thought you covered for her last night?"

"I did, and on the weekend too." She shrugged, "She's not ready to talk about it but whatever is going on with her family, I hope that everything is all right."

Stacy had not been herself lately. The usually confident friend Jodi had been accustomed too, had become distant and sometimes stand-offish. Jodi had put it down to the stress of her family situation and simply comforted her friend, doing everything she could to assist Stacy in her difficult time. Jodi couldn't count the number of times over the past few months she'd filled in for her. Not that she minded. Jodi loved her job. She loved helping people and nothing fulfilled her more than healing people and watching them come back to their full potential.

"Well, I've said it once and I'll say it again. You're a good friend Jodi. Stacy is lucky to have you." He paused, looking down at his food. "And how is Zack? Back from his trip?"

Jodi looked warily at John with a small smile. "Yes, he arrived back yesterday."

Jodi knew that John had a thing for her. Thankfully, he kept his distance and had remained professional when he had found out she already had a boyfriend. To this day John never put the hard word on her and instead had opted to become her close friend instead. She was grateful for him. He was incredibly talented, dedicated to his work, and amazingly easy to talk to. They spent so much time together that people often commented they made a good-looking couple. At first they denied it, but now they just laughed and said 'thank you' politely before walking away together. It was just easier that way, especially when no one believed them, so they just went with the flow. It had become a bit of a joke between them.

"That's good. So, any new news since last night?" John went to take another bite of his lasagna before freezing as the alarm over the loudspeaker began to blare. The doors to the staffroom burst open and Tammy flew through the doors.

"Dr. Dixon we have a gunshot wound to the chest. We need you in the E.R. immediately. Jodi we could use your help."

They both dropped their forks, deserting their dinners and ran down the hallway behind Tammy towards the E.R.

Their quiet night just got busy...

Jodi was exhausted. She looked down at the glowing dial in the dashboard of her car as she collapsed into the driver's seat. *2:50am.*

Where had the time gone?

Luckily, she didn't live too far away and the 15-minute commute to her apartment should be a breeze this time of night.

Jodi smiled tiredly to herself. The emergency bullet extraction had been a success and the gunshot patient was recovering nicely. John had insisted that Jodi aid him, and she had helped extract the bullet easily, having done it several times before. John of course, had instructed her and completed the repairs himself.

Two more patients had come into the E.R. after that, one a woman with a broken arm and the other a toddler with a high fever. She had tended to both, and now that she had come down from the adrenaline of the surgery, and the rush of the E.R. she was exhausted.

Starting the car and pulling out of the carpark, she waited patiently at the red light. As she waited for the light to change, the hairs on the back of her neck rose. She looked around uncertainly, her nerves telling her something was wrong. She reached over and pressed the central locking, feeling slightly safer, and tried to shake the feeling that she was being watched.

She gripped the wheel tightly, "Come on, come on." Jodi whispered to herself, willing the lights to change. When she saw the green, her foot went down, and she went zooming down the street. She checked her review mirror and started to relax when she saw no one was following her.

"Get a grip Jodi. No-one is after you." she reassured herself.

Letting out the deep breath she hadn't even realized she was holding, her mind quickly wandered yet again to that mysterious emptiness she had been feeling lately. It gnawed at her that she couldn't pinpoint what it was, and why lately it had become more prominent in her thoughts.

"Well, it's definitely not my work," she whispered to herself. Her job is what kept her grounded.

Was it my social life? No. Jodi's work kept her busy and social enough with her friends there. She wasn't the type to go out clubbing and to bars for a drink, so she didn't feel like she was missing out anything there.

No. It was something else.

As she drove home, the thoughts swirled around her head. Even as she ascended in the elevator to her top floor apartment, her tired mind would not rest.

As she opened her door, she was surprised to find Zack standing in the kitchen, freshly showered, a pair of trousers hanging loosely from his hips. Zack Drummond certainly fit the bill when you thought of the rich and elite, in looks and in demeanor. The tall man with a round face looked up, smiling at her as she walked in. His style-cut, brown hair falling over his face on one side, almost hiding his twinkling eyes as he looked at her.

Jodi raised a curious eyebrow, "What are *you* doing up?" Zack was usually fast asleep when she came home from night shifts.

"Couldn't sleep." Zack smiled warmly and came over to stand in front of her, taking her purse, placing it on the living room side table and pulling her into a tight embrace. "How was work?"

"Busy there at the end."

"You all right? You're later than usual." He leaned back, holding me at arm's length so he could look me in the eyes. Clearly concerned.

"Yeah. It was a good night. Everyone pulled through. I'm just tired." Jodi stood on tiptoe and kissed him lightly on the lips. "Let's go to bed."

After a quick shower, she pulled back the sheets of their supersized king bed and face planted beside Zack, completely spent from being on her feet all day.

"Just relax now. You can sleep in tomorrow." Zack's hands rubbed up and down her back.

"I know what you're doing, and it won't work." Jodi giggled sleepily into the pillows.

He chuckled lightly, "Why am I not surprised?"

"Oh, come on, you know work tires me out" Jodi groaned, as Zack's hands slid from her shoulders, kneaded down her back, and slid over her buttocks. He gave each cheek a brief squeeze before his hand ventured between her legs, massaging her sex briefly before sliding back up and continuing to massage her back.

"I know. That is why you don't have to do a thing." He gently grabbed her shoulders, flipping her over and positioned the pillow beneath her head, spreading her long strawberry blonde hair over the pillows. He lay on his side, propped up on one elbow as he looked down at her and ran his fingers through her hair.

"You really are beautiful, you know that?" He leaned down and kissed her. "Now just relax, close your eyes, and I'll help you go to sleep." He pulled the sheet across them both and disappeared beneath them. He ran his hands down her sides, until he could hook his thumbs into her panties and swiftly pulled them down free from her ankles, before positioning himself between her legs.

"Zack, I'm not in the mood. Honestly, I'm beat."

Zack's head reappeared from beneath the sheets. "I thought I told you to sleep already." He tapped her lightly on the nose. "Now close your eyes, you won't even know I'm here." He grinned cheekily.

Jodi complied, too tired now to resist and closed her eyes, leaning back into the pillows.

Slowly, Zack kissed his way down her neck, disappearing again beneath the sheets and took her breast in his mouth through her night shirt, nibbling gently at her nipple before continuing his journey down her stomach. Gently, he spread her legs wide and positioned his head between her legs, kissing her neatly cut landing strip.

"Sleep now baby." He whispered.

Jodi groaned as Zack took her clitoris in his mouth and sucked gently, before licking her from back to front several times, then sucking on her gently and swirling his tongue around her clitoris, before plunging it deep inside her rapidly as deep as he could.

Jodi fisted her hands in his hair, grinding against his face, spreading her legs wider, giving herself fully to him. It didn't take her long to find her release and as she came, she let go of his head and smiled, her eyes still closed.

"I love you Zack" Jodi whispered.

"I love you too." Zack whispered as he lay down beside her, rolled over, and immediately fell asleep.

Jodi peeked her eyes open and looked over at Zack, frowning. Something was off with Zack lately and she couldn't quite put her finger on it. She looked at the back of his head for a few moments and dismissed her concern as thoughts of that gnawing feeling came back to haunt her. Something wasn't right with her life, and Jodi pondered again what it could be as she drifted off to sleep.

Chapter Two
Dylan

♥

Dylan woke abruptly, startled. Breathing heavy as the dust floating above his head stung his eyes.

His ragged breathing slowed as he removed his fist from the hole in the wall, causing more drywall to shower down over him.

"Great. Just great!" He grumbled to himself. He quickly examined his bloodied knuckles and flexed his fingers a few times. "At least I didn't break anything this time I guess".

"Yeah, but you definitely broke this wall! Wholly hell!"

"Shane?" Dylan leaned up on his elbow and peered through the hole in the wall. It appeared that his fist had gone clean through, as he was met with the bright blue eyes of his second in command.

"Geez. Remind me not to get on your bad side Panther." He chuckled. "And remind me never to sleep against the same wall as you. A fist exploding a few inches from my face is not quite the morning alarm I was looking for."

Shane rubbed the sleep from his eyes, laughter rumbling from his throat.

"Yeah, sorry about that." Dylan raked his hand through his hair, trying to shake the last few remnant memories of his dream.

"Same one again huh?" Shane disappeared from view and came through the bedroom door a few seconds later. Dylan grunted and flopped back down on the bed, examining the large crack that made its way from the hole to the ceiling.

"Look I know it still haunts you. It haunts all of us," Shane began, "but there are just some things that are out of our control."

"Don't start with this shit again, Eagle." Dylan sat up in bed, throwing his legs over the side and hung his head in his heads, vigorously rubbing his temples as if he could rub away the memories.

"We were all there Dylan. We all share the same trauma as you. We-" Shane came to an abrupt stop as Dylan jumped to his feet, glaring at him.

"It's not the same for you as it is for me and you know it." He growled,, pointing a finger in the air at him. " I was responsible, it was my decision, it was... It was... " He dropped his hand and closed his eyes tight in frustration, "it was my fault."

The defeat in his voice at his last words stunned Shane into silence. Never had he voiced the burden he was carrying, and Shane watched as his commander and best friend, sank back onto the bed and hung his head in his hands once more.

Minutes of silence passed before Shane tentatively spoke.

"You're too hard on yourself Panther. Nobody blames you for what happened."

Dylan didn't respond. The mission playing over and over in his head.

"He's right you know." Alpha Entered the room, giving a curt nod to Shane as he passed. "But it's clear you've still got some shit to sort out." He looked at the wall behind Dylan, shaking his head with exasperation. "Go get your ass over to Grayson's." He made to leave, turning back at the door. "And stop breaking my damn walls or I'm going to start sending you the bills." With that, he strode off down the hall.

Dylan sighed. "Boy, am I going to hear it!"

Shane released a deep breath, nodding matter-of-factly. "Yep."

"I disagree." Dylan stated calmly.

"Well, you're the best we have Dylan. So, if you say you're stable, then I guess we're all good here." Alpha rose from his chair, picking up his coffee and giving a cursory look over at the medical psychologist.

Dr. Grayson crossed her arms sternly, shaking her head in disagreement.

"Look I understand your discontent here doctor." Alpha acquiesced, "but like you said, Dylan's problems off the clock have not affected his performance to date. And I too disagree with you. All you have at this stage is premonitions based off other case studies."

"No. You're making a big mistake. Clearly he has PTSD to some degree, and it needs to be rectified before he gets assigned to another mission. These night terrors are only the beginning. Soon it will impair his judgement. This is classic..."

Alpha raised his hand in the air, silencing her.

"The suspension has been denied. If Dylan says he's fine, then he's fine. I've known him a long time and I trust his judgement."

Taking a deep breath, Dr. Grayson eyed him challengingly. "Fine. Request to continue to see Commander Stevens for further evaluation."

Alpha looked at Dylan who gave a begrudging but curt nod of acceptance.

"Granted. Now if there's nothing else to discuss here, I have another meeting to attend before I head to the Pentagon."

As Alpha headed out the door, Dylan made to rise from his chair.

"We're not done here Commander", Dr. Grayson stated flatly, eying him over her glasses.

Dylan sighed and slumped back in his chair, rubbing his hand over his forehead.

"It's not that I wanted you suspended Dylan. I truly have concerns over your well-being. Your post-traumatic stress may not be affecting you now, but it might, and it may at a crucial time that also puts your team at risk. You have to understand, that what you went through was horrific. It is not something you can simply shrug off as part of the job and move on. Instances like these leave deep emotional scars, no matter how hard you try to disguise them or push them aside."

Dylan remained silent. Dr. Grayson leaned back in her chair, shaking her head.

"You said so yourself that the nightmares are getting worse and from the reports I've received, they seem to be manifesting physical violent outbursts".

Dylan looked up sharply. "What have you heard?" He asked suspiciously.

Dr Grayson regarded him coolly as if deciding whether or not to tell him.

"There have been some... reports, from some women. They are worried about you. That is all."

"They?"

"Two of your past girlfriends, or acquaintances, or whatever you want to call them, stated you had nightmares that caused you to, and I quote, "thrash around, yelling in your sleep," almost causing them injury in the process.

"Those reports must be old. I haven't slept with a woman in over nine months."

"Even so, coupled with your psych eval, you need to be extremely careful. Be mindful of your team on this next mission and keep your head clear. I want to see you again when you get back. When you do, we'll go over the progress of your current exercises."

She flicked her pen in the direction of the door, signaling she was done. Dylan eyed her warily before getting to his feet. "Understood."

As he left her office, closing the door behind him, Dylan thought about what she had said. She could be right in that he needed to deal with his issues, if not for himself, then definitely for the sake of others he gets close to. But she was most definitely wrong about it affecting his work. *No chance!* When it came to his missions, he had one hundred and ten percent focus. He had trained most of his life to be both physically and mentally superior to others. His ability to multitask, make life and death decisions instantly, and carry out missions successfully was second to none. This was why he held his position as team commander. Quite simply, Dylan loved his job, and he would not let anything, not even a past trauma, jeopardize that.

"Earth to Dylan?" A sing-song voice sang out, interrupting his thoughts. He froze as he recognized the familiar voice, and his mood sank even further as he turned to face her.

"So, I take it you've finally lost the plot then huh?" Mandy chided with one elegant eyebrow raised as she looked back at Dr Grayson's office.

Dylan eyed her suspiciously. *What was she doing here?*

She looked pretty much the same as when he'd last seen her years ago. Her long red hair was braided down one side of her head, spilling tendrils of fiery hair over one shoulder. Her long dark lashes batted over large green eyes and her lips glistened with red gloss below the small, pointed nose he had once thought was cute. Her tight, white tee shirt, skinny jeans and high heeled black boots only accentuated her tall stature, tiny waist, and long slim legs. Dylan noted that her toned body was still curvaceous in all the right places.

Damn it! She was still sexy as hell.

Keeping his thoughts to himself and exuding a look of cold indifference, Dylan ignored her, striding down the hallway and out the front doors into the bright light of the autumn sun.

"What? You're not going to talk to me now?" Mandy said with mock hurt as she followed behind him.

Dylan grunted and kept walking. "What do you want Mandy?"

"Nothing, just to say hi and 'How are you?'"

"Hi, and I'm fine. Anything else?"

"The cold shoulder then. Okay, I deserve that. I just thought that since we'd be working together again, we could catch-up, let bygones be bygones and be friends again."

Dylan halted, turning to face her. "Why on Earth would we work together again Mandy?"

"Didn't Alpha tell you?" She smiled, "The last mission I worked on involved a high-profile child. She got taken and we need her back alive, and with as little collateral damage as possible. This means you and your team."

Mandy took a step towards Dylan, reaching out a hand to caress his cheek. He tensed at her touch, but he didn't back away.

"I'm sorry for what happened between us." Mandy continued, "but we had fun, didn't we?" She drew closer, pressing her body against him and whispered, "Doesn't mean we can't again."

Dylan stared at Mandy, feeling tormented as he fixed her with a steely gaze. He knew he should have nothing to do with her, yet he couldn't deny that his body wasn't responding to her familiar touch. It had been over nine months since he had been with a woman, and he had managed to scare them all away with his tormented dreams.

Guilt stole up his spine as he recalled the fateful night he had inadvertently grabbed his ex-girlfriend by the shoulders, making her scream in pain, and threw her forcefully into the wall. A fact she had kept from Dr. Grayson. Dylan had woken just in time to see her crush against the wall, hitting her head with a thud and cutting her off mid-scream as she slumped unconscious to the floor, a trail of blood smearing down the wall behind her as she fell. Instant remorse and horror at what he had done hit him like a bullet to the chest. As he called for help and watched in a daze as the paramedics took his girlfriend from his arms, Dylan vowed he would never sleep with another woman again until he was certain his night terrors were done. He never wanted to be responsible for injuring another woman again, ever.

"I'll take that as a yes?" Mandy giggled, bringing Dylan out of his dark, spiraling thoughts. He looked at her with furrowed brows, momentarily confused, until he realized he had a hard on from Mandy pressing herself against him.

He stepped back and turned abruptly, continuing his walk towards his car.

"Hey, is something wrong?" Mandy called after him. He didn't answer. "If it's about the past, I said I was sorry."

Dylan paused, while he didn't want to indulge her or risk giving in to his physical needs, he knew better than to ignore her. His mother hadn't raised him that way. She'd always taught him from a young age to treat women with respect, even though at times it may seem hard to do so.

'Always be chivalrous, my dear. A true man must always put his lover on a pedestal, listen carefully from her point of view and show patience if she becomes your adversary, because she's most likely right.' she would say. True words of wisdom that his father had always laughed at but nodded

in agreement wholeheartedly, while enveloping his mother in his arms and kissing her. He hadn't quite understood at the time, he was only six after all, but their love was engrained in him, and he always followed their example.

He took a deep breath, getting into his car and rolled down the window to look at her.

"Look, it's not you Mandy. I just have a lot on my mind that I have to sort out. We'll catch up soon I'm sure."

Mandy didn't look convinced, but she nodded silently and waved nonchalantly at him, smiling wanly.

"I'll see you at the briefing then." She said simply.

He smiled back, grateful she seemed to understand and gave her a curt wave as he sped away from the curb. As he drove away, he groaned in frustration. He hadn't intended to run into Mandy again and he knew how persistent she could be. The woman had no boundaries. He had vowed never to get involved with her again. Not personally. Not professionally. Not ever.

Yet it seemed fate had other plans.

How was he going to get out of this one?

Chapter Three
Jodi

♥

"So how are you today?"

Jodi could hear the concern in her cousin Amber's voice and took a deep, steadying breath. Not a day went by when her mind didn't drift back to those dark days. Days of which Jodi had tried hard to forget, but no matter how hard she tried, the pain, fear, and anguish she had felt was all too much. Even though it had been years, to Jodi it felt like only last week.

"I'm fine." Jodi gulped silently. "How's things in Charity?"

There was a pause and for a moment Jodi thought her cousin would push her on her brief response.

"Great actually. The business is going really well. Tyler is turning out to be a great business partner, and together we've managed to get over a dozen new clients in the past month alone."

Amber had started her software engineering business just two years prior and it was really taking off. Jodi was really excited for her.

"Wow Amber! I'm so proud of you! You really deserve this."

"Thanks Jodi." Jodi could almost see the ear-to-ear grin Amber was wearing. "You know, if you were here, we could go out and celebrate." The hint was not lost on Jodi, and she rolled her eyes. Amber was always trying to get her to come to Charity.

"I know, I know. And I promise I will come see you soon, but you know my work keeps me busy and Zack needs me here."

There was a loud sigh over the phone. Jodi knew that Zack was not Amber's favorite person. She wasn't sure why, but when they had first met, they never got along and merrily tolerated each other for Jodi's sake.

"So how is the rich businessman?" She asked dryly.

Jodi rolled her eyes again but smiled at her cousins attempt at civility.

"He's good, although he's been really busy lately. Lots of late nights at the office."

"Has he been treating you well?"

"Yes of course. Why wouldn't he? I mean, I've moved in with him in his apartment, and he makes sure I never want for anything." Jodi smiled as thoughts of how he puts her to sleep after a long shift filled her mind. He had been doing it a lot lately, always making sure she had a 'happy ending' at the end of an exhausting day.

"Uh huh" Amber sounded skeptical.

"C'mon Amber. Cut Zack a break. What is it you don't like about him?"

"I've told you. I just don't think he's your type?"

"And what type is that?" Jodi asked dryly.

"Rich, cocky, boring..."

"Ha! Really? I think you mean, dependable, likeable... *safe*."

"No, no, definitely what I said." Amber stated. There was a pause over the line before Amber continued. "But given your history, I see why you chose a guy like him. So, for your sake, I hope he treats you right."

"Thank you, Amber." Jodi smiled.

"That being said, I still think you'd be better off with Dr. Gorgeous." she giggled.

Jodi laughed. "Not you too!" Amber had only met John on her last visit, and she had immediately swooned at the sight of him.

Amber laughed. "Oh he is definitely yummy."

Jodi checked the time on her diamond wristwatch.

"Oh, hey I have to go. Zack is taking me out to dinner."

"Uh huh." Amber grunted, her good mood evaporating in an instant.

"What?" Jodi was surprised by her reaction.

"It's just... Does he take you anywhere else? Does he plan anything different? I bet you it's one of his fundraising dinner events, where he's going just to socialize and show-off his trophy girlfriend."

Not letting on how close Amber was, Jodi sighed.

"Amber, you know he's a busy man, and I'm busy too. We don't have time to do other extravagant things. I'm fine with the dinner events, and I'm not his trophy girlfriend."

"Okay then." Amber quipped grudgingly, obviously not agreeing with her but wanting to keep the peace. "You two both have fun and I'll call you tomorrow."

Saying goodbye and hanging up the phone, Jodi looked past the expensive-looking décor and furniture in the apartment to the full-length mirror across the room. She stared at her extravagant, long, red dress with a heart neckline and split coming halfway up her thigh. The soft material reflected the light making her shimmer sultrily when she moved, and her long, strawberry-blonde hair contrasted perfectly with the red, making her blue eyes pop.

She sighed, turning away from her reflection and looked through the floor-to-ceiling height windows of the apartment that gave a spectacular view of the city below. While she enjoyed dressing up, a part of her knew this wasn't who she was.

"My god you look incredible... as always" Zack whispered as his arms slid around her waist from behind and hugged her close. One of his hands dropped to the high slit of her dress and traced a finger up to her panties where Jodi promptly swatted his hand away.

"Aww, no fun." he chuckled, kissing her cheek. Giving up his conquest, he took her hand and smiled. "Come on, let's go."

As they arrived at the fundraiser and walked around the crowd, Zack was always nearby. He hovered close, a protective hand guiding her around at the small of her back, as they greeted friends and met new acquaintances. While Jodi liked the attention and smiled politely, she couldn't help but feel alone, noticing that she was never included in the conversations that followed. Neither, she noted, were most of the other wives or girlfriends who were draped on the arms of the other men.

She also noted that Zack seemed to preen when the other men looked her up and down appreciatively, making Jodi shudder.

Was Amber right in that she really was just a trophy girlfriend?

"Is everything okay?" Zack enquired, looking concerned.

Jodi smiled and nodded, and Zack turned back to his friends. She looked around uncertainly at the opulence of the room, feeling like an imposter standing there in a designer dress. She idly wondered if she would ever get used to this lifestyle, rubbing shoulders with the rich and famous.

Suddenly, she stiffened beside Zack as she felt that all too familiar feeling, and the hairs on her arms stood on end. Her eyes darted about the room, expecting someone to be watching her. *Waiting for me*, she thought.

"Are you sure you're okay?" Zack whispered.

She opened her mouth to say something when a loud bang made her jump, grabbing Zacks arm tighter and looking around nervously.

"It's just the champagne, Jodi. Come, let's dance." Zacks grin as he led her onto the dancefloor made her relax, dismissing her anxious thoughts, and she decided to try and enjoy the rest of the night.

"You seem preoccupied this evening. Is something on your mind?" Zack led her expertly around the dancefloor, waltzing in time to the music.

"I just- I just get jumpy around loud noises."

He smiled knowingly.

"You still don't want to tell me why that is?"

Jodi remained silent and diverted her eyes, instead concentrating her eyes on his immaculately tied bowtie.

"It's okay. Maybe someday you will. But for now, let's just have some fun."

With that, Zack whirled her about the dancefloor, making her laugh as he spun her expertly under his arm several times until she was dizzy. A few dances later and both laughing heartily, they made their way back to their dinner table where their delicious looking entrees were waiting...

Zack leaned heavily on her as they took the elevator to the top floor. His lips finding her neck and nibbling his way to her earlobe.

"Zack stop", Jodi lightly pushed at his chest. "You're drunk."

"I know I'm drunk, but I also know you were the hottest woman there tonight. And I plan to do something about it." He whispered in her ear. "You've made me horny as hell all night."

Jodi rolled her eyes and pushed him away again.

"Oh, come on, stop denying me what's mine." He slurred. Reaching for the high cut in her dress again.

"Zack. Please. It's been a long night." Jodi pushed him back just as the elevator doors opened and walked out, leaving Zack to stumble out behind her, muttering to himself.

Throwing her clutch on the leather armchair, she watched amused, as Zack face planted onto the plush sofa beside it. Most times when they went out it ended in the same way, and Jodi knew that he would pass out and sleep like a baby soon enough.

"Come over here. I want to kiss the most beautiful woman in L.A." Zack called out deliriously.

Jodi laughed and sat down beside Zack, gently combing her fingers through his wavy, brown hair.

She couldn't help but wonder at how different he was to her other lovers. Never had she dated a rich, successful business type, nor did she think she ever would, but he had been so persistent in pursuing her after she had stitched a minor cut on his hand, that she had given in.

She had resisted at first, but he sent flowers to her home and a red rose would be waiting at work every day. Chocolates and spa vouchers, various gift baskets, and bottles of expensive wine were sent to her for weeks, and when she finally agreed to a date, he had given her a diamond bracelet, and the date after that, some earrings and the date after that, a necklace. It wasn't the gifts that Jodi so adored, it was the effort he had gone to, to try and please her. The fact that he had thought about her enough to always get her something. He was really easy to like and equally easy on the eyes. So *why not?* she had thought. She had wanted a fresh start after all, and it had been time for her to stop feeling down and lonely.

"Zack, do you love me?" The words were out of her mouth before she knew it.

"Huh?" Zack mumbled in a half-conscious response.

No point backing out now, Jodi thought.

"Do you love me? Like really, *really* love me?"

Zack smiled as he rolled over to look up at her, taking the hand that was stroking his hair and brushed his lips across the back of her knuckles, kissing each one tenderly.

"Why do you ask such a serious question?" He smiled up at her. "You know I love everything about you. You are the perfect woman, and I'm not the only one who thinks so." He reached up and caressed her cheek with his thumb, his eyes sparkling with glee, "Everyone was looking at you tonight, and I don't blame them."

Jodi frowned. "Zack, that's not what..."

"Sshhh" he placed a finger on her lips, looking hazily into her eyes. "I'm glad you are mine."

He leaned his head back and closed his eyes, the hint of a smile still on his face.

"One day we'll have a big family. We'll fill this place with lots of babies and be the happiest, most successful and prestigious family around."

Jodi looked down at him in shock. *Where did that come from?* They had never even discussed the topic of the type of future they would have, or even if they would *be together* in the future for that matter. They'd only been together for seven months.

"Zack, what are you talking about?" Jodi gave him a hesitant nudge when he didn't respond, "Zack?"

Zack exhaled heavily and Jodi realized he had let go of her hand and gone limp, having fallen into his usual drunken sleep.

Jodi jumped to her feet, breathing heavily as she felt the sudden rise in panic at the thought of a future with Zack.

It's not that Jodi didn't want it, it's just that she'd never thought about it. *What if she didn't want to be in the spotlight all the time, as wife to a rich business mogul? What if she didn't want the prestige that came with his name?* She was quite content with her low-profile life, away from the eyes of strangers and the world. *And babies!?*

Jodi's eyes welled with hot tears as she looked down at the handsome man, still in his tuxedo and black bowtie, who had just confessed he wanted a future with her. It was all too much to think about and too confusing to comprehend after such a big night, and admittedly, a few too many champagnes.

As the tears ran unbidden down her cheeks, she made her way to the bedroom, slipped out of her dress, and slid beneath the luxurious covers. Not caring that her makeup would stain her pillow, she leaned into it and cried.

She couldn't marry him, she knew this. Her past wouldn't let her, she was too damaged.

She sobbed, thinking about how good it would be to be married and to take on such a high-profile name and have a big family. Her mother and father would have been so proud and Zack could give her a comfortable life. A safe life.

She smiled to herself, her sobbing subsiding, as she clung to the good memories of a possible future.

However, no matter how hard she tried, it wasn't long before she started drifting to sleep, and she felt the inevitable nightmares steal back to haunt her....

Chapter Four

Dylan

♥

The hum of the helicopter blades throbbed rhythmically in the air. Dylan checked his watch. They were on time and nearly at target destination.

"Alpha one, ETA 30 seconds. Get Ready to commence drop," the voice crackled over the radio.

Dylan peered out into the jet black of the night.

"Okay, look alive everyone! This is supposed to be a quick, in and out mission. Let's keep it that way."

The helicopter began to slow, "Let's go!" he shouted above the roar of the chopper blades. He motioned for each team member to hook up and exit in rapid succession, each one hooking on to the rope and sliding down the 30-foot drop to the grassy meadow below.

The last team member hooked on, turning to grin at him.

"See you on the ground handsome." The red headed beauty winked at him salaciously before grabbing the carabiner with both hands and jumping from the chopper, disappearing over the side, and sliding to the forest floor below. Dylan grimaced. *What was he going to do about her?* Only fate and the worse luck could bring them back together. Dylan sighed heavily and plunged over the side with a final curt wave to the pilots, signaling he was the last one.

As he dropped lightly to the ground, he quickly took cover in the tree line where the rest of his team waited.

It was dark, and they had a three-mile trek ahead of them. He motioned silently for them to take formation and move out, consciously making sure he was separated from Mandy. He needed to stay focused. They were within enemy territory, and he needed to stay alert. Mandy being there was just a distraction he didn't need, but unfortunately high command thought differently, stating someone from the CIA needed to be there to confirm the Intel.

The mission was simple, locate and extract the subject. Female, 3'1" tall, light brown hair, olive skin, goes by the name of Hannah. That's all we needed to know. Who she was or why she was wanted, was none of their concern, although it wasn't hard to figure out she was important to somebody.

As they came to a clearing containing a large hunter's lodge fifteen minutes later, Dylan motioned for the team to spread out and surround the area, indicating for Mandy to stay with him. Unfortunately, she was the only one who could confirm the target. He watched diligently as his team cleared the trees and advanced on the hunter's lodge, finding refuge amongst the shrubs and dense bushes.

"Just you and me now honey," she purred.

Dylan ignored her, as the rest of the team one by one confirmed their positions around the lodge and gave the all clear.

"Mandy, can you confirm the target?" Dylan whispered as they squatted amongst the shrubbery.

Apparently, the child was to be guarded by four armed assailants, and once this was confirmed, it would be a quick and easy grab for his six-person elite team.

Adjusting her night vision binoculars, Mandy smiled at him, her white teeth flashing in the moonlight.

"I love it when you say my name." Dylan frowned at her, shaking his head as he turned his attention towards the house.

"One guard, red beenie, confirmed. No sight of the others yet." Mandy said in a low voice.

After a few minutes had passed, Dylan picked up his radio on his shoulder. "Alpha team report, do you have eyes on the potential target or assailants? Over".

"No sign of movement from the north, Panther. Eagle over."

Cobra, Cyclone and Phantom all reported nothing. It was quiet... too quiet.

Dylan clicked the radio to give the team orders to advance when Mandy suddenly grabbed his leg.

"Wait!" She whispered. "I see something. Incoming at our eleven."

Dylan adjusted his night vision goggles on his helmet, noting Mandy's hand was still on his thigh. He watched as the Jeep pulled up to the house and four armed men alighted from the vehicle. A man with a leather jacket exited the house to greet them and they all entered the house.

Dylan sighed, pulling the radio to his mouth. "Alpha team, stand down. We'll have to wait and see how this plays out. Over." With at least six men in the house, it would be harder to obtain the unconfirmed subject without one of them alerting their boss.

Dylan watched as the men appeared within view of the lit-up windows. They were discussing something urgently and it appeared they were at a disagreement.

Dylan stiffened as he felt Mandy's hand run up his inner thigh and rub slowly over his groin.

"What are you doing Mandy?" He stifled a groan as her hand massaged more urgently and his dick hardened of its own accord under the thick canvas of his military issue pants.

She shrugged, not taking her eyes off the house.

"Well, it seems we might be here a while. Why not make good use of the time?"

Dylan's eyes narrowed as she slowly undid his belt buckle, releasing the button and unzipping his fly, all the while still looking through her binoculars.

"We're here on a mission Mandy." He grabbed her arm, stilling her hand.

"That's never stopped you in the past. From what I remember you were quite good at multi-tasking." She slid her hand inside his pants before he could respond and grasped his cock, firmly rubbing up and down his shaft. Dylan groaned and let go of her arm, reluctantly conceding to her advances.

"Besides, it looks like they're getting cozy. We could be here a while."

Dylan turned his attention back to the house. Mandy was right. Leather jacket had handed out beers and most were seated around the table, deep in discussion. Dylan steadied his breathing as best he could as he spoke into the radio, acutely aware of Mandy's hand increasing in pace up and down his shaft.

"Keep your eyes peeled Alpha team. We don't move until the target is confirmed. Over."

He closed his eyes as the teams' confirmations came over the radio. When he reopened them, they were dark and heated.

He grabbed a fistful of Mandy's hair, pulling her head up from her binoculars so he could look her in the eyes.

"Don't you dare take your eyes off the house. Kapeesh?" She smiled devilishly, "Yes sir!" she slurred.

He let go of her hair and positioned himself behind her. Reaching around he unbuckled her belt and quietly shoved her forward so she fell on all fours from her squatted position. He swiftly hooked his thumbs in her pants, sliding them down around her knees with her panties, exposing her behind.

"Not a sound." Dylan hissed, as he grabbed her hips and abruptly slid into her, hesitating for a moment as he relished the feeling, before he slowly increased in tempo.

Mandy looked back at him briefly, biting her bottom lip with a triumphant smile, then turned back to look through the binoculars, grabbing the tree beside her for support as Dylan's thrusts got rougher.

"Any sign of movement?" He breathed.

Mandy stifled a moan. She knew better than to make a sound. One time she had inadvertently let out a giggle and nearly blown their cover. Dylan had not attempted to go near her for months after that, and it had made their missions much less exciting.

She swallowed thickly, "Still no sign of the target." She breathed heavily for a few moments as she scanned the building. "She must be in one of the upstairs rooms.... with the curtained windows." Mandy bit her lip from screaming out as she found her release and Dylan thrust roughly making a low guttural sound as he pulled out abruptly and came on the ground between her legs.

Mandy made to rise, but Dylan pushed her back down on all fours. "Don't move," he warned.

Mandy exhaled sharply, as moments later, Dylan unexpectedly entered her again. Her eyes left the house as she watched him feverishly relishing every ounce of pleasure.

Dylan briefly closed his eyes. *Nine months had been way too long.*

He looked up at the house, a sudden movement catching his eye. The smile on Mandy's face abruptly left as he grabbed her hair and yanked it up so she faced the house, not faltering in his tempo as he continued to take her from behind.

Mandy moaned as she focused her attention towards the movement on the second floor. "That's her, alright. She's here." she breathed.

Dylan gritted his teeth, "Then let's go get her." He was about to find his release for the second time when the sound of a branch snapping behind him made him bound off Mandy like he'd been electrocuted.

Dylan's heart beat wildly in his chest, the adrenaline pumping through his veins, as he rolled to the ground and pointed his gun at the intruder behind them.

They had been made.

Chapter Five
Jodi

♥

"Go on." John smiled up at her as he bent over the elderly patient and checked her heartbeat. "I can take it from here."

"You sure?" Jodi looked uncertain.

"Yeah, I got this." He straightened and removed the stethoscope from his ears. "Clare will be here in an hour and it's a quiet night anyway. There are plenty of other nurses that can take over if need be." He paused, looking at her with concern.

"Why are you looking at me like that?"

John crossed his arms as he examined her. "How long are you going to keep doing these double shifts? It's not sustainable you know. You look tired."

"I'm fine. Really." Jodi smiled reassuringly at him.

John didn't respond, but after a few moments nodded silently, clearly unconvinced. He looked as if he wanted to say more, but instead reached out and took the clipboard from Jodi's hands.

"Go on. Get out of here."

Jodi saluted playfully and turned on her heel down the hallway. "There's gelato in the fridge if you want it. It's your favorite!" she called back over her shoulder with a final wave.

John grinned, waving as he turned back to his patient.

Outside, Jodi did her usual quick dash to the car. Parking lots at night always made her feel uneasy and tonight was no exception. However, it felt good to be leaving early for a change. This literally never happens. She smiled to herself as she drove home, humming to the music in good spirits. She was still humming as she rode the elevator to the top floor, through the entry door, and as she treaded quietly towards the bedroom. Zack would be asleep at this late hour and all she wanted to do was have a shower, then snuggle up beside him and sleep for two days straight.

As she made her way down the hall, her humming faded. *What was that music?* Jodi froze outside their bedroom, gazing curiously at the muted light and shadows moving across the carpeted floor by the doorway. Frowning, she tentatively stepped forward, slowly becoming aware of the muffled noises and the beating of her own heart thumping faster in her ears, as she and pushed open the half-closed door.

Now it all made sense why Zack was acting weird.

Before her, the back of a naked blonde was moving sensually up and down. Her blonde hair flowing down one side of her shoulder masking her identity, until a hand reached up to caress the side of her face.

"S-Stacy?" Jodi whispered. She could not believe her eyes. Stacy, who she'd considered a friend, was riding Zack, moaning softly. She turned her head slightly at the sound of Jodi's voice and smiled at her as she continued, yelling Zack's name as she came. Zack grunted forcefully beneath her as he too came, groaning Stacy's name in return.

Stupefied by what she was witnessing, Jodi just stood there, frozen to the spot in shock and stifled a sob with her hand.

Zack's head jerked off the pillow and looked around Stacy's naked body to where she stood. His eyes went wide with horror at the sight of her and he quickly pushed Stacy off of him.

"Oh my god! Jodi!" he reached out for her, "Jodi. It's not what it looks like. I can explain!" He slapped his forehead in exasperation. "I'm sorry. It was a mistake. Please!" He jumped from the bed and hastily pulled on his boxers as Jodi shook her head and slowly backstepped away from them.

Stacy giggled, and Zack turned to her in horror. She shrugged her shoulders indifferently and rose from the bed in her naked blonde glory, looking at Jodi.

"No hard feelings, darling. I get whatever I want." She laughed smugly. "You must admit you slacked in taking care of his needs, so I simply took over."

Jodi gawked at the nurse as she very slowly commenced to put on her clothes.

"What are you doing Stacy? Get dressed and get the fuck out of here." Zack shouted hysterically.

Get out of there indeed! And that's just what Jodi did.

Quickly, while Zack continued to shout at Stacy, Jodi turned and ran out of the apartment, tears streaming down her face, her body racking as she sobbed uncontrollably. Her heart felt like it had been smashed to pieces, *again*.

She made it to the elevator doors and jabbed at the buttons. Thankfully, the elevator doors opened immediately, and Jodi jumped inside, pressing the carpark button repeatedly. She held her breath as she heard Zack yelling down the hallway, coming into view half naked as the elevator doors closed.

It was only until Jodi had reached the car and driven to her favorite place at Echo Park Lake, that she allowed herself to scream and let the heartache out.

While she had been covering Stacy's shifts, she had been sleeping with her man!?

She beat the steering wheel out of frustration a few times, before calming down and leaning back in her seat, tears streaming down her face.

"Why me?" she whispered. "Why am I such a magnet for bad luck? What have I done to deserve all the things that have happened to me?"

She sniffed, taking a few deep shuddering breaths, trying to let the despair she felt to be forgotten. Willing it away as she looked out over the waters of the lake before her that reflected the city lights, calming her. This was a place where she could think. Her special place that only her and her mother went to before her untimely death only four years prior.

"I miss you mom." She blinked back the hot new tears that stung her eyes, "I wish you were here with me. I need your guidance." She sat in silence for what seemed like an eternity, "What do I do now? Where do I go from here? I just feel like the world is closing in on me."

As if in answer, Jodi's phone vibrated. She wiped her eyes as she read the message. It was her cousin.

'Hey lovely. I know your shift just ended and I can't sleep. Any chance we can talk?'

Jodi called her immediately.

"Wow. I actually expected an *I'm too tired, I'll call you in the morning'* message" Amber chirped down the phone.

Jodi sniffed loudly, still unable to talk as she steadied her breathing.

"Jodi, are you okay?"

"A-Amber. I d-don't know w-what to do." Jodi stammered, tears coming afresh to her eyes.

"Sshhh. Calm down. Just tell me what happened." Amber's voice soothed her enough for Jodi to retell the sordid events that had transpired, and poured her heart out about being an unlovable, worthless woman, unlucky in relationships and destined to die alone.

"Nonsense!" Amber yelled down the phone. "Stop all this bullshit Jodi. It's not true. Zack is just a rich asshole who treats everybody badly. You just don't see it because he acts differently around you. He's a jerk."

Jodi thought back on the few times she had caught a few glimpses of Zack yelling, or threatening people, either in the office or in the streets when they were out. But every time Jodi queried him, he had always brushed it off with a good excuse and made light of the situation. He would always smile lovingly at her and tell her it was nothing to worry about and that it was just a big misunderstanding. She had believed him then.

Jodi shook her head and sighed. "I don't know. Maybe you are right."

"Girl, I know I'm right! And if your mom had met him, she would be telling you the same thing." Jodi smiled through her tears, nodding. She was right. Together with her mother, her aunt and Amber, the four of them did think alike and were of the same opinion.... usually. They were never shy to point out something was wrong that the others failed to see. Amber had called out Zack when they met, and Jodi had ignored it.

"Come to Charity, Jodi. I mean why not? Unless there's going to be something between you and Dr. Dreamy?" she added hopefully.

Jodi smiled. "Amber, I told you nothing can happen. We work together and I wouldn't want things to get awkward."

"Okay, okay. Worth a shot. So come here. Get a change of scenery. You have always said you love it here."

Jodi considered thoughtfully. "Amber, I..."

"No! I'm not taking no for an answer. A change of location, a new place, is just what you need. A fresh start."

Jodi sighed, "I tried a fresh start Amber, and look where that got me."

Amber groaned. "Really? You call moving to the other side of L.A. and transferring to another hospital within the same city a fresh start? Come on! That's like trying the same thing and expecting a different result!"

Jodi wiped her nose with the back of her hand, her forehead crinkling. "Hmmm. You know, I never thought about it that way." She frowned, deep in thought. "It's just, L.A. has been my home for so long, it's all I've ever known."

"I know. Look, I'm sorry I'm being so hard on you. I just want what's best for you."

Jodi giggled through her tears. "Best for me or for you?" This was not the first time Amber had asked her to come to Charity. In fact, she had been asking ever since Jodi's mother had died in the plane crash, and even more so when Amber had lost her mother, her aunt, to breast cancer.

"Both," she laughed. "Please come to Wyoming. I live in this house all by myself. Say you'll come, pretty please?" she begged. "You know our mothers would want us to be together."

Jodi sighed. *Again, Amber was right...*

Jodi thought about Amber's proposal over the next few weeks. She had been right on many things.

She had been staying at John's, having told him everything and he just nodded silently and offered a room for her to stay in until she had sorted everything out. Apparently, John had felt the same way as Amber about Zack but didn't think it was his place to tell her so. He was a true friend and gentlemen. Not like the rest of the staff.

Zack had come to the hospital repeatedly and had been thrown out by security more times than she could remember. The whisperings from the other nurses started whenever she entered a room and every time Zack came begging for her, the cold stare from Stacy, her betrayer, was too much to bear.

First thing first. She needed to cut all ties with Zack, and that meant getting all her things from his apartment. Luckily, they had only been living together for a month and she hadn't accumulated a lot of stuff. She had not returned to the apartment since that night, but decided that during the day would be okay since he would be at work.

How wrong she was.

When she tentatively opened the door and stepped in, Zack was there, drunk and half passed out on the living room floor. When he saw her, he jumped to his feet, stumbling over to grab her arm.

"You're home? Do you forgive me then?" he asked hopefully, his eyes a little unsteady. "Please. Just talk to me. I just want to talk."

"Get off of me Zack. I'm just here to pick up my things."

"No! Stay!" he begged. "Please stay. It's over between me and Stacy, I promise!"

Jodi looked down at him on his knees as he grasped her hand tightly.

"You're everything to me. I'll change. I'll be better... for you!"

Jodi's heart welled at the sincerity in his words.

Was he saying the truth? Or was he just lying through his teeth for her to stay?

Jodi looked at him uncertainly, deep in thought for a few moments.

Taking a deep breath and smiling, she grasped his hands in hers and squeezed them gently....

Chapter Six

Dylan

♥

"Look Mandy it was a mistake!" Dylan didn't know how much clearer he could be. "I apologize if I misled you. It was not my intention." Dylan paced the empty cafeteria floor in front of Mandy, who sat wide eyed with shock, saying nothing.

"I mean, we almost got caught for Christ's sake. We are supposed to be professionals. I shouldn't be distracted like that, and I hate that I was thinking with the wrong head out there." He shook his head in frustration as his pace halted.

"Say something Mandy". He looked at Mandy whose expression was slowly turning from one of shock to anger.

"It was a squirrel, Dylan." She said between clenched teeth. "We got caught by a *squirrel*!" She took a few deep calming breaths, closing her eyes momentarily before she met Dylan's gaze.

"Look, the mission went off without a hitch, right? We got the target out safe. No one got hurt... badly, and the bad guys were apprehended without raising the alarm. Mission accomplished and with a bit of fun to boot! I don't see why you're being so stand-offish all of a sudden. I thought we were reconnecting?"

Reconnecting? No chance.

They had met on the job and as a result ended up spending a significant amount of time together out of necessity. Their past relationship had been a convenience and it was a mutual understanding at the time that that was all it was. He regretted that it had gone on for so long to the point where Mandy had started to develop feelings. Being the dimwitted guy that he was, he hadn't realized it until it was too late.

"No Mandy. That's not going to happen."

"And why not?"

Dylan shook his head again and recommenced his pacing, staring at the floor with exasperation. "You've just caught me at a very bad time Mandy. I have shit I need to sort out. Besides, need I remind you how it ended?" he raised an eyebrow at her questioningly.

"So, you're saying that maybe in the future there might be a chance?"

"No. I mean maybe." He shook his head. *What was he saying?* "Look, I haven't changed my mind from back then Mandy. It's over, for good."

Mandy smiled coyly. "I understand. My poor damaged, *confused* boy." She stood, closing the gap between them and cupped Dylan's face in her hands, halting his pacing. "I have to go but thank you for helping me on my assignment. It has been fun as always." She leaned in, kissing him on the lips. "Don't be a stranger." She whispered, before she turned, picked up her jacket and left with a wink.

Dylan looked after her in confusion. *What just happened?* There's no way Mandy took the news that well.

The one thing he could give Mandy credit for was that she was one tough chick. She was one of the few women that could put up with his BS. When his dark thoughts returned, she would give him space instead of getting weird that he had spaced out. She understood him when he yelled and thrashed out at nights. Granted she had fast reflexes, that most likely helped put her mind at ease at nights. It made sense that since she was in the same line of work, that she would understand what he was going through, while other women did not. For all this he was truly grateful, but beyond that, he felt nothing but an attraction that was only physical in nature. And even then, it was only sometimes.

Dylan shook his head, freeing himself of the plaguing thoughts. At least she took it well and she was gone.

It was more than he could really hope for.

One Year Later

Nate groaned in frustration.

"Look, I know you and the boys live for the adrenaline, but there's nothing that can be done." Alpha leaned back in his chair, regarding the boys as they shuffled around uneasily. "We need time to gather more intelligence on the next mission, and it's going to take more time than we thought."

"How much time?" Nate grunted.

Alpha spread his hands, "I don't know. But look on the bright side. You guys haven't had downtime for nearly two years! Go see your loved ones, meet a girl, I don't care. Just enjoy the time away and I'll let you all know when it's time to come back."

Dylan rubbed his chin, the short beard from spending weeks in the jungle, a reminder that he desperately needed a shower and a shave.

"What are you all standing around for? Scram! Except you Dylan, I need a moment."

Shane, Hank, Nate and Colton slowly shambled out of the makeshift office. When they were alone, Alpha turned to Dylan, eying him carefully.

"How you been?"

Dylan raised a brow with amusement. "Well, I've been rolling around in mud on a jungle floor for the past few weeks. I've been bitten by critters, bruised, and bashed. So yeah, I guess you *could* say I've been better."

Alpha threw his head back and laughed. "Good. Seems like you're still your old self."

Dylan suppressed a smile. "Look, boss, if you're still worried about me, I get it. But I promise you, Dr. Grayson has worked her magic and I'm in a much better headspace."

"No dark thoughts? No nightmares?" He pressed.

"I said I was in a better headspace, not cured." Dylan chuckled.

"I see." Alpha tapped his chin with his pen, deep in thought. " Well, I guess since you're joking about it, it's not as heavy on your mind. Still, I think this break has come at a good time. Go home, see your family, fix cars like you used to. Do something you enjoy."

Dylan grunted. "I enjoy my job."

"And I don't doubt it. Maybe that's why you are the best of the best. You enjoy it *too* much." Alpha sighed. "Look just do me a favor and relax, do what normal civilians would do, and just live your life a little. Have a little fun, maybe find yourself a .... " he halted his words, second guessing his advice.

"Find myself a girl?" Dylan supplied wryly.

Alpha gave him a grin, choosing his words carefully. "If that's what you want to do, and you feel you are up to it, then why not?" He shrugged.

"You know I haven't been with a woman in a long time, and you know why. It's why I've sworn off women."

Alpha nodded solemnly. "Ok so don't. Last thing I need is for my main man to have a criminal record for accidentally putting a woman into a coma... Or worse."

"Not funny." Dylan said bluntly.

"I wasn't trying to be."

They eyed each other warily for a few moments.

"Go home Stevens."

Dylan sighed and rose from his chair. Alpha came around the desk and clasped him on the back as he walked him out.

"Say hi to Mark for me, and just have a good time, okay. That's an order."

Dylan smiled, shaking his head. "Sir, yes sir!"

"I don't believe it!"

"Yeah, well it's true. I'm coming home." Dylan scratched the back of his head as he spoke. "Not sure for how long. Could be a week, could be longer."

"Alright, alright. I'll start spreading the word. No one is going to believe me though. What kind of IT guy looks like Thor?" He started laughing uncontrollably. "This'll be good to watch."

Dylan couldn't help but chuckle and share in his brother's mirth. Admittedly, he missed his little brother and he looked forward to seeing him. That, and to give him the biggest wedgie like when they were kids, which seemed to have become a ritual in adulthood every time they caught up. As kids, Mark would try to find a way to get him back, and their mother of course, hated that she had to buy underwear every other week. As they got older, she would just shake her head when she found the stretched-out, tent-sized undies and fold them up. A subtle hint that she was no longer buying new ones. For a while they ran around freestyle, and they started pantsing each other instead. However, as young teenagers, they mutually decided one day they'd gone too far when they put an older lady into shock, and made a pact to reserve their wild antics for special occasions.

"It's a shame mom and dad aren't here. They will be devastated they missed you."

Dylan sighed. "Yeah. Unfortunately, I don't choose my holidays."

"What holidays?" Mark grunted. "I don't think your job knows the meaning of the word. I still don't believe you're coming."

"Well, let's see what your undies have to say about that."

"Oh yeah? Well, we shall see." Mark guffawed. "I hate to tell you this, but you're not that scary bro." Mark chuckled into the phone.

Dylan laughed whole heartedly grinning from ear to ear. He imagined his brother was tightening his belt as they spoke.

"Okay bro. I'm jumping on the plane now. I'll see you soon."

Nine hours later, Dylan walked off the plane, stretching his stiff legs as he waited for his bag, and went in search for a hire car.

Once on the road and hours later, he took in a deep breath as he passed the small weathered, "Welcome to Charity" sign.

I'm finally home.

He smiled to himself as the local radio blasted out some old country music, and his mood lightened considerably. It was good to be back.

He hummed to the music, drumming his fingers on the side of the open window as he entered the main street. It was getting late by the time he pulled to a stop at the central traffic light in town. Looking around, he noted with a smile the few townsfolk still lingering in the local bar and restaurants, watching their silent laughter and animated banter through the lit windows. Everyone seemed cheery and he relaxed knowing that the good little town seemed to be the same old town.

He leaned back in his seat, waiting patiently for the light to change. His fingers still drumming to the beat of the music.

"Gee, someone's in a rush." Dylan watched as a car suddenly sped through the intersection. He got a quick glimpse of a woman with strawberry-blonde hair clutching the wheel tightly in front of her as she checked her rearview mirror. A few seconds later a second vehicle whipped past.

Dylan's eyebrows raised in surprise. "For a small town, people sure still live in the fast lane around here."

For a second he thought maybe she was in trouble, but quickly dismissed the thought. This was Charity. Nothing ever happened here. The cops don't ever get called except maybe when a dog poops on the sidewalk and the owner doesn't pick it up. The most action they see is probably at the bottom of a donut box when all hell breaks loose and they scramble for a resupply. Dylan chuckled to himself at his non-sensical thinking and continued his slow drive through town, a sudden urge for donuts making his mouth water.

Pulling into his parent's driveway, he cut the head lights and coasted to a stop. The lights in the window were on but there was no sign of Mark. Grabbing his bag from the passenger seat beside him, he quietly left the car and crouched low when Mark came out onto the verandah and bent to pick up the mail.

Ha! This was too easy. There was a reason he was called Panther, and it all started from practicing on his brother for so many years. Dylan stalked up behind him unheard, chuckling inwardly at his brother's impending demise. Seeing no underwear hanging out above his shorts, he decided there was only one thing left to do.

I'm going in.

Quickly, he bound up the stairs and shoved his hand down the back of his brother's shorts to find the doomed garment.

Yelping, he pulled it out abruptly.

The feel of a creamy, textured substance was all over his hand. He held it up, looking disgustedly at the brown mush between his fingers.

"Is that ... is that... shit?" he gasped in horror.

Chapter Seven

Dylan & Jodi

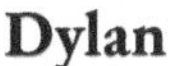

Dylan

He looked disgustedly at his hand, wiping it furiously on Mark's shirt. "Dude. What the...."

Mark laughed harder, gasping for air.

"Bro, the look on your face," he gasped. "Priceless!" he burst into a new fit of laughter.

Dylan sniffed his hands, frowning. "So help me god, if this is..."

"Whoa, Whoa. Hold your horses," he chuckled. "It's just crunchy peanut butter. I thought I'd be prepared, go commando and set a trap while I was at it," he grinned.

Dylan's face slowly broke out into a grin. Shaking his head, he took his brother in a big bear hug, clapping him on the shoulders.

"Alright bro, you win this round."

Mark hugged his brother back, just as eagerly.

"Dude, you're crushing me." Mark spluttered after some time. "Do me a favor and lay off the gym while you're here."

Dylan let him go, laughing and looked around the front porch. "It's good to be home. I'm looking forward to the downtime."

"Even in no action charity? I give you three days before you start getting jumpy and restless." he challenged.

Dylan chuckled, shrugging his shoulders. "Maybe."

He couldn't deny his brother was right. If he were out of action for too long, he became restless and couldn't calm down. He did love coming back to see his family though. It was a rare occasion.

"How is Uncle Dave?"

"He's actually not feeling well, but he'll be all right. He's got a nurse who sees him at the house now. He seems to be happy with her." Mark leaned up against the porch railing studying his brother, his arms folded. "I'm more interested in how you are though?"

Dylan smiled wanly at the concern in his brother's eyes. "I'm fine."

Mark nodded. "I can only imagine what you're dealing with bro. The shitty things you've seen, the people you've lost. I definitely couldn't do your job." His voice dwindled out, deep in thought. "I know there's only so much you can tell me, but if you ever want to talk about it, you know I'm an inexperienced ear you can rely on that will take your secrets to the grave, right?"

"Thanks bro." Dylan laughed. "Duly noted."

"I know! Let's go hit the bar in town. Maybe you might even meet a pretty little lady to take your mind off things."

"No! No women." Mark watched as Dylan tensed visibly.

"Whoa. Okay. Okay. Down boy. No girls it is. You want to tell me about it?"

Dylan eyed him steadily, making Mark hold up his hands in resignation. "So that's a *no*," he said with mock caution. "Still up for a beer?"

Dylan shrugged. "Sure."

"Great. First things first. I need a shower bro, cause crunchy peanut butter butt-crack is not pleasant!"

Dylan chuckled, his demeanor suddenly changing. His brother always had a way of cheering him up. He followed his brother into the house and looked around the homely living room of his parents' house.

It was good to be home.

He sank into this father's comfy armchair as he waited for his brother to get ready.

Maybe being here could help him let go of his dark memories. Maybe he might even let go of the notion that he was responsible and forgive himself for what happened.

All he knew is that he couldn't let his guard down around women yet, and they were definitely off the table. Especially in his home town. The last thing he needed was to burn bridges *here* of all places.

He shrugged the notion off. *Why am I even thinking about this?*

It was highly unlikely he would meet anyone any time soon, especially in this small town.

Least did he know that destiny had other plans for him, and his soulmate was closer than he thought....

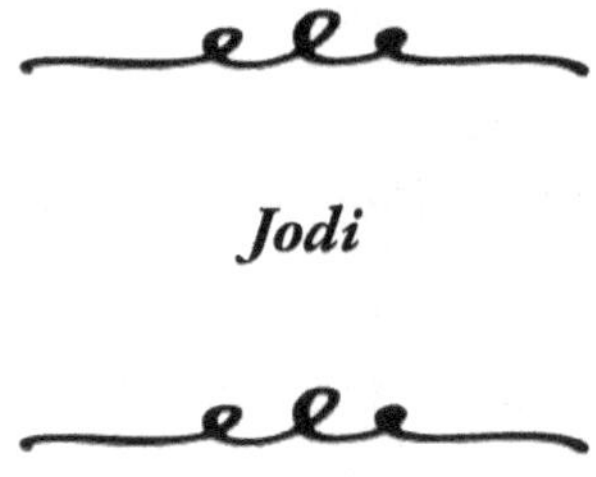

Jodi

Amber was right. She had needed a completely fresh start. New scenery, new people, new job.

It felt good to say good riddance to Zack Drummond for good. She'd packed her bags and left without a second glance back. She promptly went back to the hospital and handed in her resignation and gave John a big hug goodbye. Deep down Jodi knew that John wanted her to stay but she couldn't bring herself to do that. There was nothing else good here for her.

As she had driven out of the huge city, the wind whipping through her hair, she had looked back at the city's reflection in the rear-view mirror.

"Goodbye, my sweet city. Until next time," she had whispered and smiled as she felt the weight of the world lift from her shoulders.

She had decided it was time to let go of her past. Let go of the fear and stop it from controlling her. Even though she had not felt that feeling of someone watching her for some time, it had felt good knowing she would be far, *far* from the past drama of her life. Finally, she felt like she could escape her past, escape the darkness.

This was something she should have done a long time ago, and even though she had been in picturesque Charity for a year now and still missed the hustle and bustle of city life, she liked the simplistic lifestyle the small town offered. She had no regrets.

Amber had been overjoyed, cried, and had all but mauled her to the ground the moment she stepped from her car. She enjoyed the fact that now they could talk over hot chocolate late into the night instead of over the phone.

"Oh, how I wish our moms were alive to see this. They would have loved to see us living together like this." Amber had cried.

Jodi took a deep breath, smiling to herself as she thought fondly of her cousin. She loved her dearly, despite her repeated attempts for matchmaking, even when Jodi had vehemently sworn off men and had told her so many times. Even so, she wasn't blind to the wandering eyes and the kind gestures from men of the town towards her. She just couldn't let her guard down again. Not yet anyway.

Maybe some day she would be ready and that someone out there, some smart, kind, *faithful*, strong man would love her back, and would hold her, protect her, and keep her safe from all the nightmares of her past that refused to let her go.

While the change of scenery had been the best decision of her life, no matter how hard she tried to forget, no matter how hard she tried to put all the heartache behind her, the pain of the past kept creeping back. Sometimes at night when all was quiet, its black tendrils would grip her heart, causing the fear to return and the panic to climb up her throat... paralyzing her.

What am I doing? Stop it Jodi!

Jodi hastily shook away the unpleasant thoughts and stared out the window at the quiet town.

If it weren't for Amber's invitation to come to Wyoming over a year ago, Jodi didn't know where she would be right now. Her new job in the small hospital was great, and she loved all the staff there. Everyone was so friendly and helpful.

Jodi's thoughts were broken by the sudden bright light in her rear-view mirror. She squinted as she tried to look over her shoulder at the car that had pulled up behind her, trying to see the driver, but to no avail.

"Easy Jodi. It's just another car," she whispered like a mantra to calm herself.

Despite her efforts, she couldn't help the thumping in her chest that gradually got louder and louder, and the hairs on her arms suddenly stood to attention. That feeling that someone was watching her was back full force. She had felt it a few times at work only recently but had shaken it off as impossible and just her imagination, but now she was not so sure.

She pulled slowly out of the parking space and out onto the road, watching fearfully as the car followed her.

Trying not to panic, Jodi sped up trying to lose them on her way home. She watched in horror as the car followed her every turn. She sped up more, zooming through the intersection in town, trying to fight back the panic that threatened to overtake her, and figure out her options for help.

She felt the fear set in as her heart thumped rapidly in her chest and the panic rose in her throat.

"Oh no," she whispered frantically. "No. Not again....."

To Be Continued...

Get Book 1 -
Fighting Temptation

♥

Enjoyed this prequel?
Get Book 1 in the *Fighting For Love Series* and see how our lovers meet.

https://getbook.at/FightingForLoveBook1

<u>Fighting For Love Series</u>

This is a Small Town Romantic Suspense series where not everything is as it seems. Our Heroine Jodi is a nurse from the bright lights, trying to escape her past in small town Charity. What she doesn't know is that trouble will find her in the form of our protective alpha, Special Forces Hero, Dylan, who has some dark secrets of his own.

If you like feel good romances made from unexpected encounters, then you will love reading the passion, temptation and suspense in this series by Aaliyah Rose.

Warning! This series does get a bit steamy.

Book 1

A big city girl. A mysterious stranger... An irresistible attraction.
The small town scenery is a welcome change from the lights of the big city.

Jodi, a talented and skilled nurse, has moved far from all the heartache and the gossip of her past... Or so she thought. All she wants to do is help people heal, lead a peaceful life and to be left alone.

However, the small town won't give her her privacy and an unexpected encounter with a masculine stranger threatens to upheave her quiet plans.

Dylan's home for a short time, a break from his perilous job. His concentration is purely on his work and he's sworn off women... At least until he can escape the darkness of his past.

When he meets Jodi, she takes his breath away, but she's not giving him the time of day. She's over men, especially the mercurial, mysterious ones, that seem to just want one thing. Yet their attraction to each other is undeniable.

Will they drop their guards and give in to the passion that threatens to consume them? Or will they let their pasts continue to haunt them?

Fighting Temptation is Book 1 in the Fighting For Love series. A small town romance where not everything is as it seems. If you like feel good romances made from unexpected encounters, then you will love reading the desire, drama and temptation in this novella by Aaliyah Rose.

Get this contemporary romance filled with heated temptation today! ♥

Follow her on Facebook: @AaliyahRoseRomance

https://www.facebook.com/
AaliyahRoseRomance

Please Leave A Review

♥

P.S. Readers,

I thank you sincerely for reading the prequel to the Fighting For Love series. I hope you enjoyed it as much as I enjoyed writing it.

From a young age I grew up amongst the pages of a book, an eager little bookworm that would literally consume all genres of fiction books. I would immerse myself in the different worlds that were created by various authors and I would get lost in them for days. Reading so much made me want to be a writer, especially when a purely good book would leave me thinking about it for days afterwards.

So, as an author new to the scene of publishing, my readers are my inspiration. When I read your reviews and hear your thoughts on my book, it helps me to continue my passion of writing while getting better at it. This means I can improve *to give my readers the best experience. And don't forget that leaving a review also helps fellow romantics like yourself decide whether the book is right for them. Reading reviews certainly helps in this area.*

So, if you feel so inclined, please leave a review on your preferred place of purchase. It would mean a lot to me.

I thank you kindly, and I'll see you in the next book...

Aaliyah xoxo

Other Books by Aaliyah Rose

♥

My Merry Commando
Book 3 coming December 2022

<u>Forever Soulmates Series</u>
Eternal Spark
Book 2 coming soon

Check out Aaliyah's books on her website:

https://aaliyahroseromance.com/books

About The Author

❤

Book lover and daydreamer Aaliyah Rose found her love of writing at a young age but didn't start publishing until recently. She writes passionate, suspenseful romances that pull the heart strings and always ends with a happily ever after.

As a newer author to the scene, your support is her inspiration. Aaliyah is excited to have you read her books, with her aim to provide heart-warming romances that will make you smile and of course, create those sexy and charismatic book boyfriends to satisfy her fans.

Aaliyah Rose currently lives in sunny Australia and when she isn't dreaming of romance, she enjoys getting out and about in nature with family and friends. If she's lucky and her two toddlers are not jumping all over her, she enjoys staying in and watching movies over a steaming mug of coffee and some sweet and salty popcorn (although

Nutella on bananas and strawberries is fast becoming a new favourite).

Email: Aaliyah@AaliyahRoseRomance.com

Follow or Like @AaliyahRoseRomance

https://www.face-book.com/AaliyahRoseRomance

9 798846 167315